You Made Me a Mother

WRITTEN BY Laurenne Sala   ILLUSTRATED BY Robin Preiss Glasser

HARPER
An Imprint of HarperCollinsPublishers

You Made Me a Mother
Text copyright © 2016 by Laurenne Sala
Illustrations copyright © 2016 by Robin Preiss Glasser
For information address HarperCollins Children's Books,
a division of HarperCollins Publishers, 195 Broadway, New York, NY 10007.
www.harpercollinschildrens.com
Library of Congress Control Number: 2015932001
ISBN 978-0-06-235886-8
The artist used ink and watercolors to create the illustrations for this book.
Typography by Jeanne L. Hogle
18 19 20   PC   10 9 8 7
❖
First Edition

To my mom, Mambert, and to all the other
best moms in the world.
—L.S.

Special thanks to Boba baby carriers and Futuristic Films for
making this book come alive in the first place.

To my Sasha and Ben, who transformed me.
—R.P.G.

I felt you.
You were a pea. Then a lemon. Then an eggplant.

I followed advice.

I read twelve books.

I ate lots of spinach.

Could you tell I was nervous?

I talked to you. Sang to you.

I wasn't sure I was ready.

But then you were here.

Ten toes. Eight pounds.

Love.
Big fat love.

I rocked you.

I held you.

I fed you.

I realized that I would spend my
life doing things to make you happy.

And that would make me happy.

Sure, there are times I still get nervous.

And times I don't have the perfect answers.

But then you smile. And
you say my name.
    You grab my hand with
those little fingers.

And I remember that everything is magic.

If I could,

I would open my heart,

and love would rain down all over you.

And you would giggle.

And I'd do it all over again.

And we would walk, hand in hand.

Until you let go.

I made you, but you made me a mother.